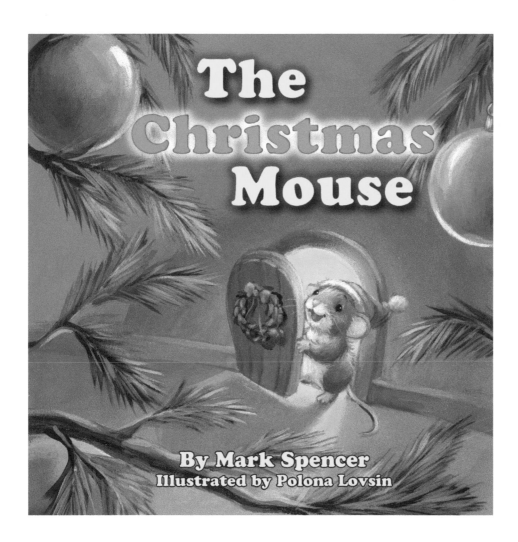

The Christmas Mouse

By Mark Spencer

Illustrated by Polona Lovsin

Halo ●●●●
Publishing International

ISBN 13: 978-1-61244-488-8
Library of Congress Control Number: 2016913239

Printed in the United States of America

Published by Halo Publishing International
1100 NW Loop 410
Suite 700 - 176
San Antonio, Texas 78213
Toll Free 1-877-705-9647
www.halopublishing.com
www.holapublishing.com
e-mail: contact@halopublishing.com

Halo
Publishing International
www.halopublishing.com

To all who love Christmas

May this simple story add to the delight

of your celebration of His birth

To Mom and Dad

Thank you for making the season magical

To Kurt, Kole, Nathan and Mason

The torch is passing – keep the magic alive

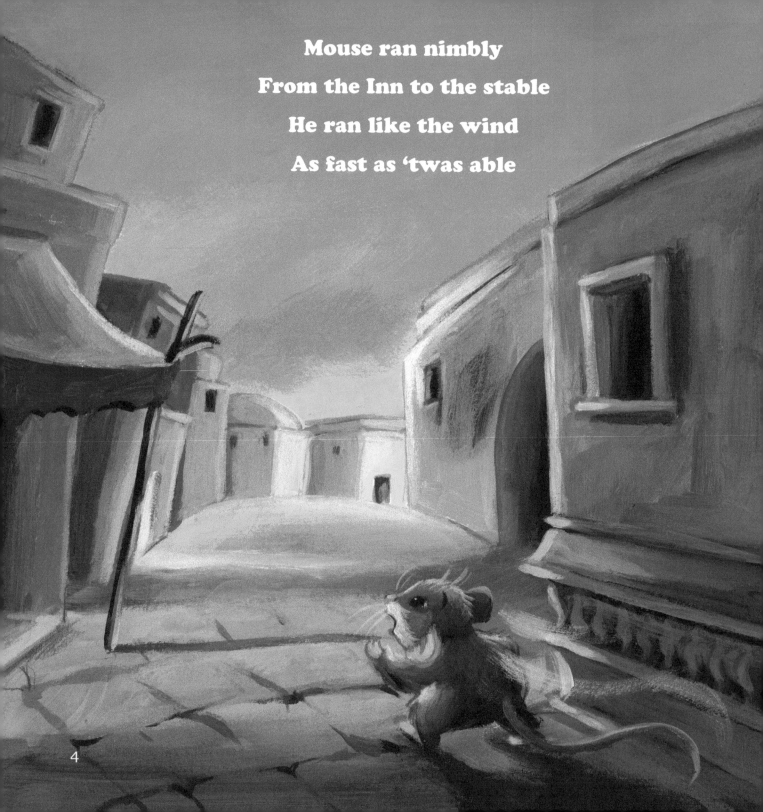

Mouse ran nimbly

From the Inn to the stable

He ran like the wind

As fast as 'twas able

He ran past Goat
He ran past Sheep
He ran under Donkey
Up the rail he did leap

Quiet Mouse cried

Will you listen to me?

I have wonderful news

My friends harken and see

The animals hushed
They grew quiet and still
And Mouse told them all
The good news with a thrill

Tonight in our home
Wondrous things there will be
A man and a woman
Will soon become three

How can this be?

They asked as Mouse smiled

And told them the lady

Would soon bear a child

The animals gasped
And then burst into chatter
Whatever is wrong asked Mouse
What's the matter?

I'm certain groaned Camel

Of losing my stall

For surely they'll take it

The biggest of all

I'm certain groaned donkey
Of losing my hay
For surely they'll take it
A soft place to lay

I'm certain groaned Sheep
Of losing my wool
For surely they'll take it
To clothe the babe full

I'm certain groaned Goat
Of losing my milk
For surely they'll take it
To feed their young ilk

Before Mouse could answer

A great light did appear

And the voice of an angel

Said hush, do not fear

This night is a night
Like none ere before
And many shall travel
Near and far to adore

A king with no crown

He'll be worshipped by three

Led by a star

Bearing gifts shall decree

That this child to be savior
Is sent for us all
Certainly Camel you could
Lend Him your stall?

18

For all of mankind
Down his life he will lay
Certainly Donkey you could
Lend Him your hay?

Worthy, Beloved
The Word made full
Certainly sheep you could
Lend Him your wool?

20

Anointed, Redeemer

Of those you call ilk

Certainly Goat you could

Lend Him your milk?

Then Donkey then Camel
Then Sheep and then Goat
All shook their heads no
And the angel did note

That four had been asked
Out of five that dwelled here
For something they cherished
Something held dear

The angel then turned to

The fifth brown and furry

And as he leaned close

He presented this query

Tell me then Mouse
For the time draws nigh
What would you share
With the one most high?

Mouse looked at angel
And he wanted to speak
But no sound came forth
No not even a squeak

The angel's head bowed

And he sighed heavily

I'm saddened in each

And now I must leave thee

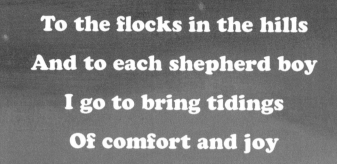

To the flocks in the hills
And to each shepherd boy
I go to bring tidings
Of comfort and joy

Then his smile it did quicken

And his eyes they did dance

And he laughed as he offered

Them all a last chance

Is there none here among you
Who will give up their bed
A place for God's chosen
To lay His sweet head?

Not I said Camel

And not I said Sheep

Nor I said Donkey

All Goat did was bleat

Then Mouse humbly spoke
Sir take this old manger
My home I do offer
A gift to this stranger

The angel's face beamed
And it gave off great light
This pleases the One
Who has sent me this night

From the heart you gave all

When the rest could give none

And so it is written

For God's only Son

A promise He makes
As His grace does begin
A door to each home
Where believers dwell in

Through them each season
Pass through to the Living
Reminding the world
Of God's Spirit of Giving

For from this day forward
In each faithful house
You shall be known
As the Christmas Mouse

The Tradition

As the Christmas season approaches, create a new tradition in your home by leaving Mouse a door to enter and bring the blessing of the Spirit of Giving, a reminder of what we truly celebrate - the birth of the baby Jesus, God's gift of Himself to all of us, that we might live with Him forever.

You could leave this book against a wall near your tree, or on the mantel of your fireplace, or any place everyone can see it to help keep the focus of the holiday.

You could move it each night and see who finds it the next morning. A small finder's prize could add to the fun.

You could make it a project for the family this year and build your own door for Mouse from craft materials, or maybe get out the art supplies and draw and color a door, or even several, for Mouse to use throughout your home.

Have fun, be creative, and have a Merry Christmas!

How does your family celebrate Christmas with Mouse?

Tell us your story at www.TheChristmasMouse.com.

CPSIA information can be obtained
at www.ICGtesting.com
Printed in the USA
BVHW020020190122
626509BV00002B/48